## About the Author

Robyn Pager, the author of *The Weeping Wizard*, lives in London where she grew up with a large family full of children of all ages. Robyn graduated from Huddersfield University where she studied English Literature & Creative Writing. She started writing poetry and fantasy fiction before she had the epiphany to pen a children's book inspired by her love of magic and the children in her family.

The Weeping Wizard

**Robyn Pager**

# The Weeping Wizard

Nightingale Books

NIGHTINGALE PAPERBACK

© Copyright 2021
**Robyn Pager**

A CIP catalogue record for this title is
available from the British Library.
ISBN 9781838750565

*Nightingale Books is an imprint of
Pegasus Elliot MacKenzie Publishers Ltd.
www.pegasuspublishers.com*

First Published in 2021

**Nightingale Books
Sheraton House Castle Park
Cambridge England**

Printed & Bound in Great Britain

# Acknowledgements

I have to start by thanking my father, Ryan, always supportive of everything I do. My mother, Sharon, and her partner, James, for funding my love of books and encouraging me to pursue writing and finally my amazing grandparents, Shirley and Dennis, the core of my family who always loved having all the grandchildren over!

Once upon a time there was an enchanted kingdom called Nitania.

Nitania was full of witches and wizards, fairies and dragons, and all other manner of magical creatures who lived together in harmony.

In this kingdom there was a school where all the children born to be witches and wizards learned to do magic. It was named the Fasinare Academy.

One such boy at this school was Jasper. However to all of his classmates he was nicknamed the Weeping Wizard because whenever he couldn't do a spell he would start to cry. As Jasper wasn't very good at magic this happened often and the other children would always laugh and tease him.

On one particular day at school the teacher, Miss Aster, was trying to teach them how to turn a pillow into rabbit. She told them that the magic spell was Verto-Lepus. You had to say it as you waved your magic wand from left to right.

A boy named Marcus waved his wand as he shouted, "VERTO-LEPUS!" and his pillow became a big fluffy white rabbit that took up the whole table!

Then a girl named Scarlett said, "Verto-Lepus," but all the pillow did was grow a pair of furry pink bunny ears and feet.

But no matter how many times Jasper tried, the pillow wouldn't change. Soon he was the only one in the class not to have transformed the pillow. So, he started to weep.

There was a song the children would sing whenever little Jasper started to cry and so, Marcus sang,

*"Is that wailing I can hear?*
*It's exactly as I feared.*
*The Weeping Wizard can't do magic,*
*It's oh so very tragic!"*

And the rest of the class laughed at the poor Weeping Wizard.

Just then, the bell rang and Miss Aster told them all to stop laughing and that it was time for lunch. But the Weeping Wizard remained in class for he was still very upset.

Ever since he was a little boy, Jasper wanted to be the best wizard there ever was but he just wasn't good enough. He could never do a spell right. So, while everyone else was having their lunch he sneaked out of the front gates of the school.

Jasper travelled down to the small wizarding village in Nitania to ask all the witches and wizards how they got to be so magical.

First, Jasper went to the market place. There he saw the potion master demonstrating his new potion for super-strength to a crowd. It was green and bubbly with smoke coming out of the cauldron.

The potion master picked a man in the crowd who took a sip. The man walked over and picked up a horse and carriage with his bare hands and lifted them above his head! Jasper, fascinated by the little show, went up to the potion master and asked, "How did you get so good at potions, sir?"

"I practised very hard at the academy every day and at home," he replied. "Potion lessons were my favourite classes so I was always very good at it. But I did well in my other subjects too because I was happy."

Jasper thought for a second about what his favourite class was. He soon realized none of them were because he was always scared he would do something wrong and that everyone would laugh and sing at him. At finding no help from the potions master, Jasper continued down the market.

After a while Jasper saw the Magical Creatures shop, famous for selling all kinds of animals, and decided to go in. There he saw phoenixes, three-headed dogs, trolls and loads of little fairies. He also saw MissBeasta stroking one of the unicorns. He ran up to her as she started whispering to it.

"What did you say to the unicorn, Miss Beasta?" he asked.

"I asked her to be careful the next time she goes racing with her brother," she said.

"How does she know what you said?" he asked again.

"I've always been very good with animals and I enjoy looking after them," she said. "At the academy I studied hard in the Care for Creatures class because I wanted to work with animals but it wasn't easy. I was always asking the teacher for help when I was stuck and bought loads of books too." She quickly said goodbye to Jaspar as she said it was time to feed the baby dragons.

Jasper left the shop thinking about what he would like to do when he was older. "Maybe I could be an animal keeper... Oh but I don't like animals bigger than me," he thought. "I don't know what I want to do because I'm not good at anything!" he said to himself.

At finding no help from Mrs Beasta, Jasper set off down the road again.

Further into town Jasper saw the Astrology School and decided to go inside. All around him there were witches and wizards looking through gigantic telescopes at the sky. Jasper didn't know what Astrology was so he went up to one of the wizards and asked.

The young astrologer replied, "Astrology is looking at the stars, then trying to work out what they tell us about the future. You will study it in a few years' time at the academy," he said. "I was okay at other classes but I knew I would be good at astrology because I wanted to learn about the future."

"Is astrology hard to learn?" asked Jasper. He really wanted to know about his future.

"It's very hard but I made some friends who also liked astrology and we would work together all the time to see if we would get the same answers. We always helped each other if someone was stuck too," answered the astrologer.

Jasper said thank you as he left the centre, head dropped down on his chest. He thought about what class he had friends in but he realised that he didn't have any friends. So he went to the steps by the wishing well and began to weep.

"I'll never be a great wizard," he sobbed. "I don't have a favourite class, I don't know what I want to be when I'm older and I don't have any friends!" he cried.

"JASPER! JASPER!" a girl shouted. "JASPER!"

Jasper raised his head. It was the girl Scarlett from his class. He sobbed, "Hi, Scarlett. What do you want?"

"We've been looking for you everywhere! Where have you been?" she asked.

Jasper told her about his day in the market place and finally said, "So I'll NEVER be a great wizard!"

"Oh Jasper," Scarlett said, "you've been listening to the wrong parts of their stories!"

"What do you mean?" he croaked.

"Well, the potion master said he practised every day at school and at home. Do you practise at home, Jasper?" she said.

"No, I never thought to work at home," he said.

"And Mrs Beasta said she studied hard in class and she would ask the teacher for help. You never ask Miss Aster for help, you just start weeping," Scarlett replied.

"But, no one else asks for help, they can always just do it," Jasper hiccupped.

"Not everyone is the same, Jasper, some are better at others in different things. Like the astrologer, he knew he would do better in a class when he did something he liked and he made friends in that class who he could ask for help."

"But, I don't know what I like and I don't have ANY friends!" the wizard wept.

"I'll be your friend, Jasper, all you have to do was ask. Have you asked anyone to be your friend?" she asked.

The young wizard shook his head. "When you can't do a spell and start crying without asking others for help, sometimes people might not want to talk to you. If you ask one of us for help instead you might get better and make some friends!" Scarlett took him by the hand and said they should get back to school because everyone was worried about him.

"Thank you for helping me, Scarlett," Jasper said.

"That's what friends do, Jasper, I'll help you as much as I can," she replied.

Once Jasper was back at school, he did all the things he learned from the witches and wizards from the town with his new friend Scarlett's help. He asked his teacher Miss Aster for help when he couldn't transform his pillow. She told him he had been waving his wand the wrong way so when Jasper shouted, "VERTO-LEPUS!" this time his pillow turned into the biggest rabbit in the whole class! And everyone clapped and applauded.

At home time, he asked his mum if on the way home they could get some books for him so he could learn more. So, she took him to the library where they borrowed some books and later that evening he practised a spell to wash the plates.

He tried over and over again until he did it all on his own!

As a reward the next day his parents brought him a broomstick!

And when Jasper was at school, he asked his new friend Scarlett for help on spells and soon he became the best in the class! He started to help others when they were stuck too and everyone became his friend.

But best of all, Jasper, the weeping wizard never wept again. He was always smiling with his new friends and he soon became to be known as the very whimsical wizard!